# The Mystery of the Round Rocks

# The
# Mystery
# of the
# Round Rocks

by MARK MEIERHENRY and DAVID VOLK

Illustrated by JASON FOLKERTS

SOUTH DAKOTA STATE HISTORICAL SOCIETY PRESS   PIERRE

This publication was funded, in part, by the
Great Plains Education Foundation, Inc., Aberdeen, S.Dak.

The authors would like to acknowledge Craig Volk, assistant professor, Department of Theatre,
University of Colorado at Denver, for his invaluable assistance in the writing of this book.

Library of Congress Cataloging-in-Publication Data
Meierhenry, Mark V.
The mystery of the round rocks / by Mark Meierhenry and David Volk ;
illustrated by Jason Folkerts.
p. cm.
ISBN 978-0-9777955-3-6
1. Glacial epoch—Juvenile literature. 2. Glacial erosion--Juvenile
literature. 3. Rocks—Juvenile literature. I. Volk, David, 1947- II.
Title.
QE697.M515 2007    551.7'9209783—dc22
2007014581

Printed in Korea

11  10  09  08  07   2  3  4  5

*Dedicated to all stewards of the land, past, present, and future*

# The Mystery of the Round Rocks

A long time ago . . .

Before time was kept, a tall peak soared above the other mountains. The weather had been warm, but it was growing cold. A crack opened in the mountain top. Each year it got bigger.

One day the crack split open, and the top of the mountain crashed to the valley floor. The rock formed a cave where a saber-toothed tiger found shelter.

Each year the weather became colder. An ice age was beginning. Soon a layer of ice formed on the stone. It crept up and around the fallen mountaintop.

The ice became a glacier. It carried the fallen mountaintop with it across many miles. The glacier broke up the stone as it moved. It ground it down into hundreds of smaller rocks.

One day the glacier began to melt. It left rocks and boulders behind on the prairies of South Dakota . . . a mystery left behind in stone.

Max and Hannah loved to visit their grandparents' farm in South Dakota.

The twins fished in the stock pond and played with the dog, Scout. They saw deer running across the prairie and pheasants flying up from cornfields.

Max and Hannah even liked helping with the chores. Their ancestors had been doing the same type of work for a hundred years.

One day they found a huge pile of rocks in a corner of the field. Hundreds and hundreds were stacked up in the shape of a tepee.

"I bet Indians did it, or aliens," said Max. Hannah was not so sure, especially about the aliens.

"Hey, look—they are all as round as bowling balls. How did that happen?" Max wondered.

"Let's ask Grandpa," Hannah said. They found him in the shelterbelt.

"Well, where have you two been while I've been planting trees?" asked Grandpa.

"We found a pile of round rocks," announced Hannah. "Max thinks the Indians or maybe aliens put them in piles, but I don't. What do you think, Grandpa?"

"Let's go have a look and eat our picnic lunch," Grandpa answered.

They walked over to where the round rocks were stacked. As they ate, Grandpa began to explain.

"The story of the round rocks began long before the Indians lived here. It was a time when winter lasted almost all year long. The frozen snow piled up a quarter of a mile high—taller than any building in Chicago or New York. And the ice was not only piled high, it actually moved across the land."

Max and Hannah stopped eating. They looked at each other. Was Grandpa joking? He often did.

"Remember last winter when it snowed three feet and the wind howled for weeks?" he asked. "We could walk on the hard snow from the house to the barn, remember?"

They nodded.

"But then what happened?" Grandpa asked.

The twins looked at each other. Was this a trick question?

"It melted," they said together.

"That's right," said Grandpa. "Spring came and the ice melted."

They all laughed as they remembered when Max slipped. He had plopped down with a thud into the mud of the farmyard.

"In the ice age," Grandpa said, "spring almost didn't come at all. Summers turned cool. Up north, it got so cold that the snow stopped melting. It started to build up into sheets of ice.

"This build-up caused pressure on the bottom. The ice squirted out as if you put a tube of toothpaste on the ground and stepped on it. Squish, squish."

"Yuck," said Hannah.

"Cool," said Max.

"The ice and snow became a great frozen river called a glacier. It crawled across the land an inch at a time."

"Many years passed. The glacier covered thousands of miles. As it moved, it leveled everything in its path.

"It took the tops off mountains, wiped out forests, scooped up tons of rock, sand, gravel, and dirt. It rubbed off the sharp edges of the rocks until they were smooth and round. When the glacier finally reached our farm, it was humongous.

"It was a rock-filled, dirt-filled, tree-filled ice cube!"

The twins chuckled. Only Grandpa would call a giant iceberg an ice cube.

"Why did the weather change?" Hannah asked.

Grandpa munched on his sandwich. "Scientists really don't know for sure," he finally said. "But they have some ideas."

"Tell us, Grandpa!" they begged.

"You kids know that the earth rotates and orbits the sun. That it kind of 'wiggles' as it goes through space, right?"

Hannah and Max nodded.

"Most scientists think that sometimes the earth's path around the sun changes. Some parts of the world get less sunlight. Springs and summers get shorter and cooler. The weather turns frigid for many years.

"Other people also think that ocean currents and active volcanoes can change the weather."

"There have been many ice ages. The glaciers of the last one stopped right here on our farm," Grandpa said.

"How do we know the glaciers ended here?" Max asked.

"Imagine a gigantic iceberg sitting just across the river," Grandpa pointed. "Imagine that the weather finally warms up. Water drips off the iceberg. Year after year, the glacier sheds tons of water.

"The water makes a small ditch for itself. The ditch becomes a little stream and finally a large channel. That channel is now known as the Missouri River."

"I always wondered why the river was so cold," Max said, shivering.

Grandpa laughed. "Another sign that the glaciers ended here is the land itself," he added. "Last year we went on two road trips, remember?"

"Sure. We went to Minneapolis to see the Vikings and the Green Bay Packers play in the dome," Max replied.

"What did we notice as we drove east from here?" asked Grandpa.

"The land was as flat as a pancake," said Max. "I wondered where kids could find a hill big enough to sled on."

"What was our other road trip?" Grandpa asked Hannah.

"To the Black Hills to see Mount Rushmore," she replied.

"And what was the land west of here like?"

"It was very hilly. The Black Hills seemed more like the Black Mountains to me," Hannah added.

"Correct you are, clever girl. Some people think the land is different because of the glacier. It flattened one side and left the other upright. The river is the dividing line."

"Grandpa, how did the animals survive when it was so cold and icy?" Hannah asked.

"The animals learned to eat foods that would grow in the cold climate. They were bigger, too, and they had warm coats. One elephant-sized animal looked like a shaggy mop. Any guesses what it was?"

"The wooly mammoth," both twins shouted. They had visited the mammoth site in the Black Hills. The animals had been stuck in the mud of a water hole thousands of years ago.

"That guy knew how to grow a fur coat!" chuckled Grandpa. "He also had a hump on his back so that he could store food—he always had his picnic basket with him."

The twins laughed.

"There were giant deer, bison, tigers, and wolves, too. Nastiest of all was the short-faced bear. Only his face was short. He stood over eleven feet tall and weighed as much as a car. If he stood up, he could look right into your window in the farmhouse, Hannah."

Hannah shivered at the thought.

"Now, what animal haven't I mentioned? It was puny compared to the other animals. It had only two legs and could not run fast. It didn't have a fur coat to keep it warm. Any guesses?"

"Humans!" the twins said

"That's right. Humans lived during the last ice age. They had to be clever to survive. They hunted the big animals to get fur coats for themselves. They built houses out of furs, ice, and dirt. They invented weapons from rocks and bones.

"They also had fire. They used it to keep warm and to cook their food. They ate meat, vegetables, and fruit like we do, but they didn't have cavities. Do you know why?" Grandpa asked.

The twins looked sheepishly at each other.

"Because they didn't eat candy?" the twins ventured.

"That's right. When kids finished a meal there was no dessert."

"Grandpa, you haven't told us how the rocks got here," Max said.

"As the glacier melted, it left behind the dirt and rocks it had picked up along the way. Billions of gallons of melted water kept the rocks tumbling along in streams and smoothed them."

"But how did they get stacked up like that?" Hannah asked.

"Your great grandparents came here from Europe to find a new life," Grandpa reminded them. "They found round rocks scattered all over this farm. They picked the rocks up and stacked them here so they could plow the land."

Grandpa stood up and dusted off his lap. "We better get back to work," he said. "Your grandma will think we have been sleeping when she sees how little we've done."

As he and Max walked away, Hannah picked up one of the smallest rocks from the pile. The smooth round rock was no longer a mystery for her. It was all that remained of that mountaintop picked up by the glacier so many years before. She tucked it into her pocket as a memento of the ice age and of Grandpa's farm.